# in the
# Tomb of Ice

T0327796

Written by Chris Bradford
Illustrated by Korky Paul

# Collins

## The Jungle

Jake Jones, the famous treasure hunter, trekked deeper into the jungle.

"Are we getting close?" asked Jen, the scientist on the expedition.

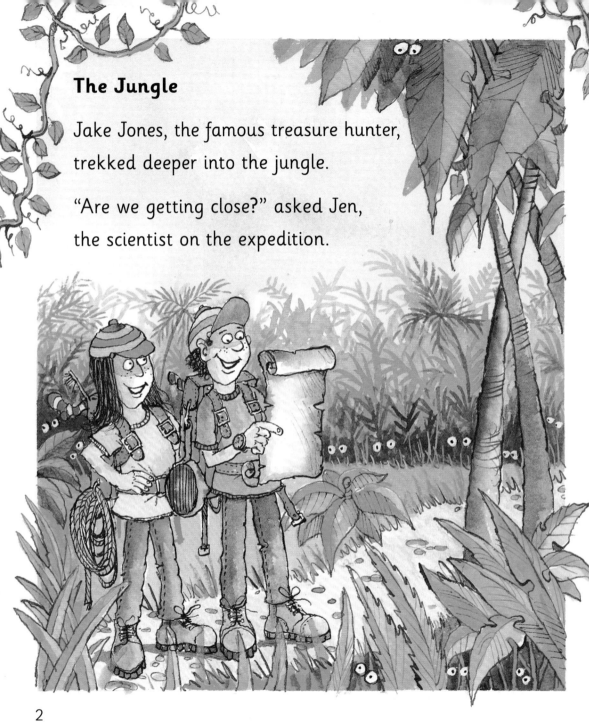

Jake checked their position on the map.
"The tomb should be across this river."

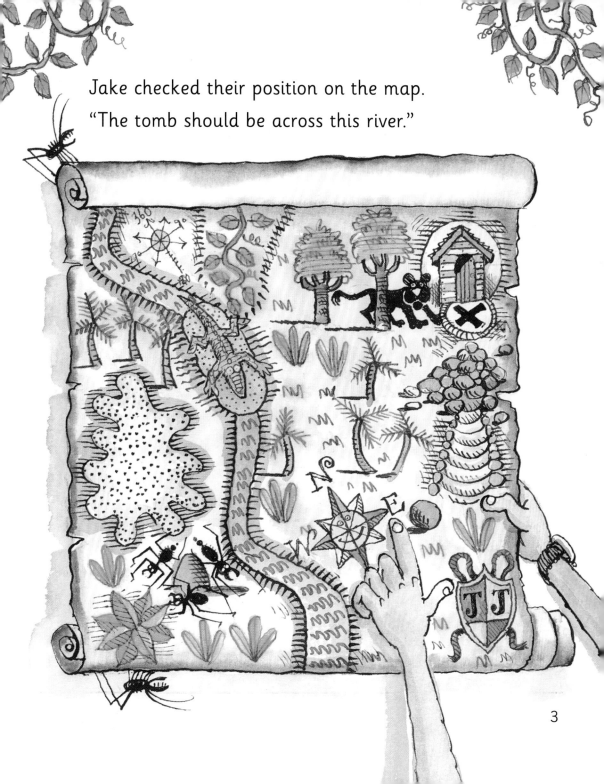

Jen winced from a bite to her leg.

"Army ants!" she cried.

Jake felt ants crawling over him too.

He brushed them off, but others came swarming from the bushes. "Run!" shouted Jake.

They fled into a clearing. "That was nasty!" said Jen.

Suddenly she leapt away and pointed to the ground. "Quicksand!"

Jake's feet were sinking fast. Jen took a rope from her knapsack and threw it to him. She pulled him to safety.

"Treasure hunting is dangerous work," said Jake with a grim expression.

They hiked on until they came to a river.

"We'll have to swim," said Jen.

"No, look!" Jake pointed to an alligator in the water.

"We must swing across."

He nodded at a vine hanging from a tree.
"You go first." The alligator snapped at Jen's heels,
but she landed safely.

Jake then swung over the monster's
gnashing teeth. "See you later, alligator!"

### The Tomb of Ice

Jake found the entrance to the tomb behind a gnarled tree. Entering, they saw a huge white casket shining in the darkness.

"The treasure must be in there," whispered Jake.

"Then let's hurry," said Jen.

10

"Wait!" Jake shouted, spotting a jaguar asleep on a ledge. "That's the gatekeeper of the ice tomb."

They crept past the jaguar to open the casket ... but froze as a large black spider scuttled across. "I hate spiders!" Jake hissed.

"They don't scare me," said Jen and wrenched open the casket.

A bright light filled the tomb and a blast of cold air made them shiver. Inside the casket, red and green ice jewels sparkled.

Jake and Jen grabbed one each.

"Should we save another?" asked Jen.

"No time!" Jake replied.

"The tomb is closing on us!"

## The Close Escape

With the ice jewels in their possession,
Jake and Jen raced out of the tomb.
But they woke the jaguar. It leapt
from the ledge and gave chase.

Jake and Jen swung back across the river.
The jaguar jumped over in one bound.

"Quick, up there!" Jake shouted. They climbed a rock face to escape.

But at the top Jen knocked a boulder loose.

The huge rock rolled towards them.
Jake and Jen slid down a canyon to get away ...
and landed in a heap at the bottom.

A shadow loomed over them. They looked up to see their arch-enemy, Shane.

"Hand them over," said Shane. Behind him stood his henchman, Vincent, cracking his knuckles. Reluctantly, Jake and Jen gave them the ice jewels.

"You'll regret this!" promised Jen.

As Shane and Vincent walked away sniggering, a voice shouted, "Shane! I told you *not* to take ice lollies from the freezer!"

Jake and Jen turned to see their mother striding across the garden. They chuckled as their older brother got told off ... instead of them!

"Sweet!" said Jake.

"And ice lollies are even sweeter!" replied Jen, taking some out of her pack.

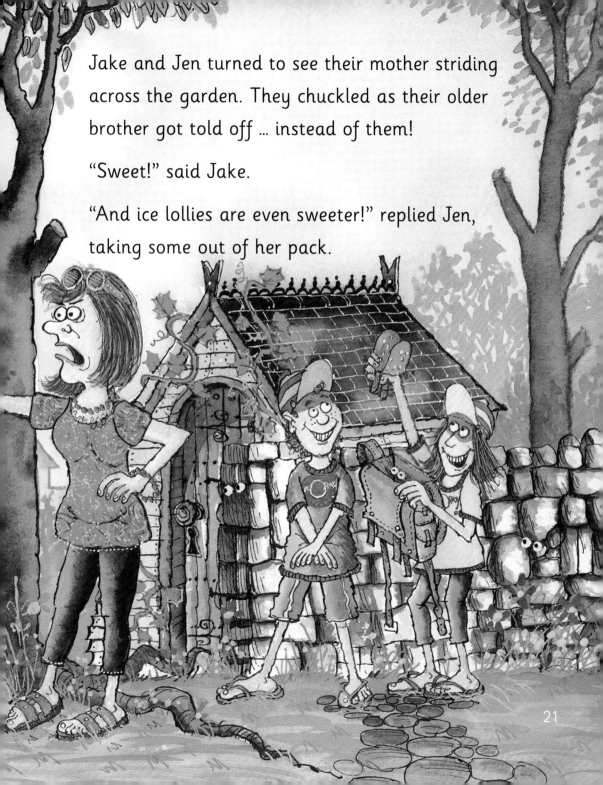

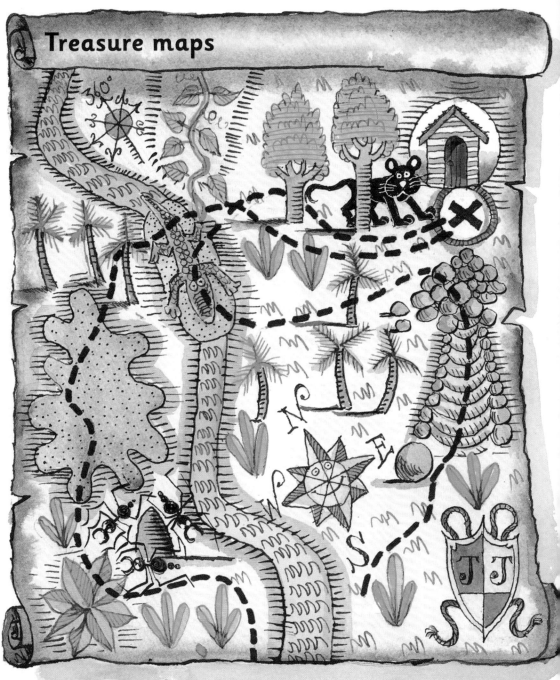

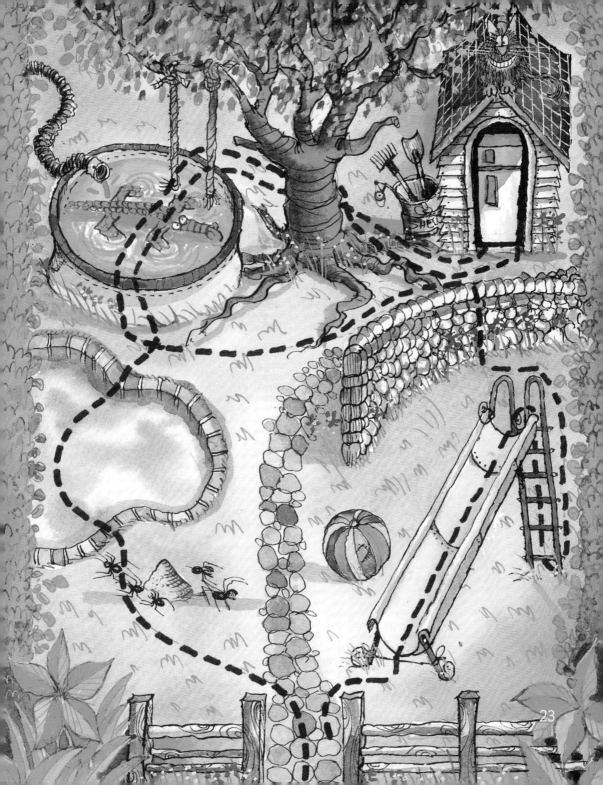

# ♟ **After reading** ♟

**Letters and Sounds:** Phases 5–6

**Word count:** 519

**Focus phonemes:** /n/ kn, gn /m/ mb, /r/ wr, zh /s/ sc, ce /sh/ ti, ssi /zh/ su

**Common exception words:** of, to, the, into, are, said, were, one, their, water

**Curriculum links:** Geography: Physical geography, Geographical skills

**National Curriculum learning objectives:** Spoken language: listen and respond appropriately to adults and their peers; Reading/Word reading: apply phonic knowledge and skills as the route to decode words, read accurately by blending sounds in unfamiliar words containing GPCs that have been taught, read common exception words, read other words of more than one syllable that contain taught GPCs, read aloud accurately books that are consistent with their developing phonic knowledge; Reading/Comprehension: understand both the books that they can already read accurately and fluently ... by making inferences on the basis of what is being said and done

## Developing fluency

- Your child may enjoy hearing you read the story. Model reading dialogue with expression.
- Now ask your child to read some of the dialogue with lots of expression, particularly focusing on lowering their voice at pages 10 and 11.

## Phonic practice

- Point to the word **knapsack** on page 6. Ask your child to sound out the word and blend the sounds together **kn/a/p/s/a/ck**. Can they point to the grapheme that represents the /n/ sound in this word? (*kn*)
- Do the same thing with the word **gnashing** on page 9.

## Extending vocabulary

- Ask your child to spot the synonyms below. Which is the odd one out?
  - shiver      sparkled      shone      (*shiver*)
  - jumped      woke      leapt      (*woke*)
  - tomb      rock      boulder      (*tomb*)